KT-232-510

ABERDEEN
CITY LIBRARIES
www.aberdeencity.gov.uk/libraries
Aberdeen City Council
Cornhill Library
Tel. 696209

Return to ....

or any other Aberdeen City Library

Please return/renew this item by the last daye shown Items may also be renewed
by phone or online

1 7 SEP 2012	2 4 SEP 2015
	1 0 NOV 2015
1 8 OCT 2012	3 0 NOV 2015
1 5 APR 2013	
1 0 NOV 2014	
2 4 NOV 2014	WITHDRAWN
3 0 MAY 2015	
2 3 JUN 2015	

X000 000 040 9841

ABERDEEN CITY LIBRARIES

For Dylan, Arlene and Dante

LENNY HAS LUNCH copyright © Frances Lincoln Limited 2009
Text and illustrations copyright © Ken Wilson-Max 2009

First published in Great Britain in 2009 and in the USA in 2010
by Frances Lincoln Children's Books, 4 Torriano Mews,
Torriano Avenue, London NW5 2RZ
www.franceslincoln.com

All rights reserved

No part of this publication may be reproduced, stored in a retrieval system,
or transmitted, in any form, or by any means, electrical, mechanical,
photocopying, recording or otherwise without the prior written permission
of the publisher or a licence permitting restricted copying. In the United Kingdom
such licences are issued by the Copyright Licensing Agency, Saffron House,
6-10 Kirby Street, London EC1N 8TS.

British Library Cataloguing in Publication Data available on request

ISBN 978-1-84507-979-6

Illustrated with acrylic on canvas

Set in Bokka-Solid

Printed in Heshan, Guangdong, China by Leo Paper Products Ltd. in August 2010

3 5 7 9 8 6 4 2

Lenny Has Lunch

Ken Wilson-Max

F

FRANCES LINCOLN
CHILDREN'S BOOKS

Lenny is in
the kitchen
with Daddy.

Lenny plays with his bear.
Daddy chops vegetables.

potatoes

onion

celery

carrot

tomato

Daddy chops onions, tomatoes, potatoes, carrots, and celery.

"One, two, three and in the pot!"
says Daddy.

"One, two, three and in the pot,"
says Lenny.

Daddy and Lenny sing.
Wilbur howls.

"Row, row, row your boat!
Gently down the stream.

Merrily, merrily,
merrily, merrily,
life is but a dream."

Lenny points.
"Food's ready!" shouts Daddy.

Daddy says, "Lunchtime!"
Lenny says, "Lunchtime!"

Daddy puts Lenny in his chair,
and ties his bib.
Lenny says, "Lunchtime!"

Lenny takes a spoonful of food.
Lenny opens wide.
Splash! On the table.
Lenny takes more food.
Slurrrp! In his mouth.

Splash!
Slurrp!
Slurrp!
Splash!
All gone!

"What a dirty face,"
says Daddy.

Daddy gives Lenny
a yoghurt.
Lenny sucks and spills.
Suck! Plop!
He licks his lips.

Daddy takes Lenny
out of his chair and
gives him a tickle.
Lenny laughs.

"All finished?" asks Daddy.
"Mmmmmmmmm", says Lenny.
"All finished!"